"As the curious little possum, Opie, hangs on a tree by his tail, so will the reader hang on every word as Jamey M. Long weaves a tapestry of cleverly written and captivating imagery in *A Possum's Gold Rush and His Discovery of the American Frontier* that will leave you spellbound as it entertains your curiosity and enriches your mind. Through Opie, Jamey sheds light on the hardships endured by the pioneers as well as the thrill and excitement that drove the gold rush across the American Territory to California. Opie's clever whit and his unwavering loyalty to those he cares about reinforces his generous spirit as Opie gains deeper insight into the history of America and helps the boy and his family find gold. The kindhearted nature of Opie, the boy and his family will warm your heart and their generosity knows no bounds. Readers of all ages will richly be rewarded for joining Opie on his gold rush adventure, which conveys a powerful and inspiring message that is more precious than gold."

–Melissa D. Reedy
The Free Lance-Star

D0061668

A POSSUM'S GOLD RUSH

AND HIS DISCOVERY OF THE

AMERICAN FRONTIER

A POSSUM'S GOLD RUSH

AND HIS DISCOVERY OF THE

AMERICAN FRONTIER

written by Jamey Long

TATE PUBLISHING & *Enterprises*

A Possum's Gold Rush and His Discovery of the American Frontie
Copyright © 2009 by Jamey Long All rights reserved.

This title is also available as a Tate Out Loud product. Visit www.tatepublishing.com for more information.

No part of this publication may be reproduced, stored in a retrieval system or transmitted in any way by any means, electronic, mechanical, photocopy, recording or otherwise without the prior permission of the author except as provided by USA copyright law.

The opinions expressed by the author are not necessarily those of Tate Publishing, LLC.

Published by Tate Publishing & Enterprises, LLC
127 E. Trade Center Terrace | Mustang, Oklahoma 73064 USA
1.888.361.9473 | www.tatepublishing.com

Tate Publishing is committed to excellence in the publishing industry. The company reflects the philosophy established by the founders, based on Psalm 68:11,
"The Lord gave the word and great was the company of those who published it."

Book design copyright © 2009 by Tate Publishing, LLC. All rights reserved.
Cover & Interior design by Stephanie Woloszyn
Illustration by Brandon Wood

Published in the United States of America

ISBN: 978-1-60604-771-2
1. Juvenile Fiction / Historical / United States / 19th Century
2. Juvenile Fiction / Animals / General
08.12.08

DEDICATION:

This book is dedicated to Mrs. Miller. Even though she left this world too early, she left behind so much goodness and joy. Thank you for being my Kindergarten teacher and teaching us all so much. Your memory will always be with me. May God bless you.

the corner of the room. He scurried across the floor and hid behind the chair.

"I have packed all of the food for our trip too," said the boy's mom. "I just need to put the food into the wagon."

"I will help you with the food, Mother," said the boy. "Go on out to the wagon and I will be right there."

Another adventure, thought Opie. *I knew the boy would be doing something exciting.* Opie loved an adventure and wanted to go along with the boy and his family. However, he did not have much time. When the boy turned to close the window, Opie ran across the floor to where the food baskets were sitting. As Opie approached the food baskets, he could smell the wonderful food waiting inside. Opie was always hungry and he could not resist the smell of food. He raised his big furry nose and took a great big *sniff!* He found the basket that smelled the most delicious and climbed inside. "This is a good hiding place," said a chuckling Opie. "No one will ever find me in here." Just as Opie climbed inside the food basket, the boy walked over, picked up the baskets, and carried them to the wagon. The boy then climbed up the wagon and sat with his

O n the edge of a small northern town there was a forest. It was December 5, 1848, and a possum was waking up to a full moon during a cold winter's night. Opie the possum hung by his tail on a big branch high above the ground. He stretched out his arms and legs and let out a great big yawn. He untangled his long pink tail from his favorite branch and began climbing down the tree to the ground far below. Opie looked up at the full moon through the trees and the forest around him. *Another beautiful night,* thought Opie. *It is a perfect night to go for a long walk through the forest.*

Opie began walking through the forest. He passed many of his forest friends who were playing in the woods. He began thinking about his other friends outside of the forest, the boy and his family. Opie had become very fond of the boy and always had a fun time when he visited him. They always had some sort of an adventure. The boy and his family lived in a town not too far from Washington, D.C. *If I walk all night I might arrive at the boy's home by morning,* thought Opie. The thought of seeing the boy made Opie very happy, and he

9

quickly began scurrying through the forest. Opie traveled all night until he reached the boy's home.

The sun began shining from behind the tall green trees. Opie took a moment to look at the beautiful sunrise and then headed across the boy's backyard to his porch. Opie crawled up onto the porch. He saw that the back door to the boy's home was open. Opie could hear the boy and his mother and father talking inside, so he poked his head inside to see what was going on.

"Finish getting everything ready, son," said the boy's dad. "We do not want to be late."

"Everything is ready, Father," replied the boy. "The wagon is packed and all of the horses are fed and ready. We can leave for Washington, D.C., in a few minutes. I am excited. I have never been to the nation's capital before!"

I wonder what is going on here, thought Opie. *Why are the boy and his family packing up all of their things? And why are they going to Washington, D.C.?* Opie, a very curious possum, decided that he needed to get a closer look to see what was really going on. Opie quickly snuck inside the boy's home and looked for a safe place to hide. As Opie looked around, he found a rocking chair sitting in mother and father. The father snapped the reigns, and the horses began walking down the old dirt road. They were on their way to Washington, D.C.

The boy and his family continued traveling down the dirt road all morning. *We have been traveling quite a long time,* thought Opie. Just then the wagon stopped. Opie, still hiding in the food basket, could not contain his curiosity anymore. He had to know where they were and what was going on. Opie carefully raised his head out of the food basket to look around. "It looks safe," said Opie as he quietly climbed out of the basket. Opie crawled over to an opening in the back of the wagon. He looked outside only to see the boy and his family walking down the street.

Opie did not want to be left behind. He climbed out of the back of the wagon and followed the boy and his family. As they walked down the street, Opie was amazed at everything he saw. There were many large buildings, but one particularly stood out. It was a big white building with a dome on top of it. The building also had giant pillars in front of it, and steps that led up to the tall doors in the center of the building. Opie had never seen anything like it before. *I wonder what this building is,* thought Opie.

The boy, his family, and Opie walked closer to the building. "Is this the capital building?" the boy asked his father.

"Yes, son, it is," replied the boy's father. "This is where all of the decisions are made for America by Congress and the President. Now, let's get inside. We do not want to miss what the President has to say to Congress and the people."

Opie was glad the boy had asked what the building was. Even though he was a very smart little possum, he had never seen anything like this building in the forest where he was from. "If the boy and his family traveled all this way to hear what the President has to say to Congress," said Opie, "it must be really important."

The boy and his family climbed the stairs to the U.S. Capital and went inside. Opie quickly scurried behind them before the big wooden doors closed behind them. As they walked through the rotunda, Opie looked up and saw how beautiful it was. The dome was lit up and the top of it was painted. "This is a very special place," said Opie. "Many wonderful things must happen here."

The boy and his family continued walking down the hallway. They made their way to where

Congress meets and then sat down in the chairs behind all of the congressmen. Opie did not want to be seen. He climbed on top of one of the flag poles hanging in the back of the room so he could watch what was going on.

"We will now come to order," said a tall man with a commanding voice. The man wore a dark suit, white shirt with a high collar, and a tie. The man also had long gray hair that was combed back over his head.

"Yes sir, President Polk," replied one of the congressmen and the room fell silent.

"As many of you know," continued President Polk, "the United States of America is growing. In 1803, we gained the land west of the Mississippi from France in the Louisiana Purchase. Over the past two years, we have also gained Nevada, Utah, Arizona, New Mexico, and Texas from Mexico. Through the Treaty of Guadalupe Hidalgo, we also acquired the California Territory for fifteen million dollars and ended the war with Mexico.

"The main reason that I am addressing you all today is to talk about California," said President Polk. "There are rumors that there is gold in California."

"Are the rumors true?" asked another congressman. "If the rumors are true, why would Mexico sell us the land instead of keeping all of the gold for themselves?"

That is a good question, Opie thought to himself.

President Polk paused for a moment. "The rumors are true," President Polk finally replied. "I believe that Mexico did not look for gold since they already had several productive gold, silver, and copper mines in Mexico. On January 24, 1848, gold was officially discovered at Sutter's Mill. James W. Marshall was working at the mill, and he found small pieces of gold along the American River.

"I would like to have volunteers to head West to California to prospect for gold and to create new towns and colonies. What you find there will be your own. This will be a very long and tough journey, but it will mean a great deal to the development of America. Do I have any volunteers?"

The boy's father stood up and said that he and his family would volunteer to go to California. Many other people in the crowd also stood up and volunteered to leave their homes and travel out West. Congress and the crowd began yelling and cheering at the discovery of gold and the development of California. Opie could not contain his excitement and also let out a big *Hooray!* He then climbed back down the flag pole and followed the boy and his family back to their wagon. Opie took one last look around before crawling back into the wagon where he would not be seen. They were now on their way to California.

The boy, his family, and their furry friend Opie traveled west through Virginia, Kentucky, and into the Missouri Territory. After a long journey through Missouri, they finally reached a small town called Arrow Rock. Once in Arrow Rock, the boy and his family arrived at the Santa Fe Trail. The Santa Fe Trail would take them through the rest of the Missouri Territory and closer to California. The boy pulled out a map. "According to this map," said the boy to his father, "the Santa Fe Trail has two routes that we can take. There is the Mountain Route and also the Jornada Route."

Opie, being a curious possum, wanted to look at the map to see where the two routes led to. Opie climbed the tree that was nearby and hung down by his tail above the boy and his father. From above, Opie could see the map and both routes clearly.

Both routes traveled west along the Arkansas River and then led into Kansas.

I wonder what route we should take, Opie thought to himself as he studied the map.

"The Mountain Route is longer but is less dangerous," said the boy. "It is closer to water and there are also less warlike Indians than the Jornada Route."

"Then it's settled," said the boy's father. "We will go on the Mountain Route first thing in the morning."

Good idea, thought Opie. He then climbed back down the tree and headed back to the wagon. The boy and his family were tired from the long day's journey. "This looks like a good place to cook supper and make camp for the night," said the boy's father.

Opie was glad to hear that because he was very hungry and tired from riding in the back of the wagon. His stomach was growling so loud he was afraid someone would hear it and find his hiding place. The boy helped his father make a fire and to set up the tent for the night. The boy's mom began stirring the pot hanging above the fire with a big wooden spoon and then filled everyone's supper dish. Opie could smell the beans and meat cooking over the fire, and his stomach could not resist the temptation any longer. While everyone was eating their food and having a wonderful time singing songs, he quickly scurried over to the pot of food that was now sitting and cooling by the campfire. Opie leaned over the edge of the large cooking pot. He put his furry snout inside and ate the rest of the food. When he was done eating, his belly was full and he let out a great big burp.

Opie then waddled over to a nice spot in the tall green grass where he would rest during the night. Opie lay on his back and looked up at the clear night sky. He thought about how beautiful and quiet it was, and how it reminded him of home. He was very glad to be going with the boy and his family on this special journey. Opie was very tired. He knew he had to get some rest because tomorrow would be a long day traveling on the Santa Fe Trail. Opie was soon fast asleep.

The next morning Opie and the boy's family loaded up their wagon and continued down the Santa Fe Trail. They traveled to Fort Osage, Independence, and then into Kansas City. Suddenly the boy's father stopped the wagon. "This is a very special place," said the boy's father. "Do you know what this place is called?"

The boy thought long and hard. "No," finally replied the boy. "What is this place called, and why is it so special?"

As smart as Opie was, he also did not know where they were or why it was so special, but he was eager to find out. "This is called the 'Heartland,'" said the father to his son. "It is called this because it is the middle of America."

"The middle of America!" exclaimed Opie, "This is a very special place." Opie thought about how far that they had traveled, and also about how much farther they had to go. He then realized how large America was and how grateful he was for the country he and the boy lived in. Opie wanted to get a better look around. He climbed on top of another tall tree by the wagon to take a look around. As he looked around, Opie saw nothing but blue sky as far as the eye could see. He saw mountains, hills, vast prairies, and herds of buffalo all around roaming in the distance. Opie also saw Native Americans, or Indians, living in peace and farming their land.

After a short break, they continued traveling

through Kansas and soon came to a new trail. The trail was called the Oregon Trail. "I wonder if the Oregon Trail will take us to California?" said Opie. The boy pulled out the map from his back pocket and took a long look at it. "The map says that the Oregon Trail will take us close to California," said the boy. "We are definitely going in the right direction." Opie was glad to hear that, and he was very excited to help get the boy and his family safely to California.

Opie, the boy, and his family continued down the Oregon Trail. They followed it through Kansas, Nebraska, Wyoming, Idaho, and finally into Oregon. Once they arrived in Oregon, Opie and the boy's family took the Siskiyou Trail into California, which led this special group into a small town called San Francisco. San Francisco was known as a boomtown because of all of the people who set up camp in search of gold. "We are finally here," exclaimed a very excited Opie. He then climbed out of the wagon and began following the boy and his family, who were already walking through the streets in town.

As they walked through town, they passed schools, churches, blacksmiths, and several other merchant stores that sold gold mining supplies to the "forty-niners." "Forty-niners" were early pioneers who gave up their homes to come to California. Many of them came by covered wagons, and some came by ships to mine for gold and to help build the towns. Most were Americans. However, as Opie could tell by observing the people around him, "forty-niners" were also people who ventured to California from Europe, Latin America, Asia, and Australia.

The boy and his father walked into the store to get some mining supplies. Opie was not far behind. As the boy pushed the door open, Opie snuck inside. "Welcome," said the store owner to the boy and his father. "What can I do for you?"

"We would like to get some mining supplies," replied the boy's father.

"I see," said the store owner. "I think I have just what you need." The store owner grabbed a sack full of pans, tools, and lanterns that were all used for mining. He then sold them to the boy and his father. The boy and his father left the store, with Opie close behind. They headed back to the wagon and put their new supplies inside. Opie crawled back in the wagon as well. They began heading

down the road that led to their claim where they would mine for gold.

Once they arrived at their claim, Opie got out of the wagon and looked around. He saw a cave in the side of a large hill and a large riverbed next to it. The boy and his father unpacked their new mining equipment while the boy's mom began setting up their new home. The boy's mom fixed them some food. She was making Miner's Griddle Cakes that tasted a lot like pancakes. They boy and his father ate them before they went to work mining for gold. Opie also managed to find a way to sneak a few griddle cakes for himself before he was off to search for gold too.

"Let's start by the river," said the boy's father. The boy grabbed a pan and began scooping sand from the riverbed. Once the sand was in the pan, the boy and his father shook the pan. Shaking the pan caused the sand to sift through the small holes, leaving only the larger rocks or minerals in the pan. The boy and his father did this for quite a long time, but did not find any gold. Opie was sad to see that the boy and his dad had not yet found any gold. Even though they had not found any gold, they were having fun finding some other interesting rocks and minerals. "I must help them find the gold," exclaimed Opie.

Opie took another look at the large cave. He began walking toward it. "I bet there is gold in the cave." Opie walked into the cave. The cave was very dark, but this was not a problem for Opie. Possums are nocturnal animals and can see everything in the dark. As Opie walked through the cave, he began to see little shiny yellow objects all along the walls of the cave. Opie walked closer to one of the shiny yellow objects and tried to pull it out with his paws. Opie pulled as hard as he could, but it just would not budge.

Opie had an idea. He decided to use his tail to try and pull it out. Opie took his long pink tail and wrapped it around part of the shiny yellow object. Opie pulled so hard that the shiny yellow object went flying out of the cave wall, landing outside the entrance to the cave.

"What was that?" asked the boy and he turned to look at the cave where Opie was inside. "I am going to go for a closer look." The boy went over to the cave entrance. He looked down at the ground and saw the shiny yellow object. It was gold. He picked up the piece of gold, lit his lantern, and walked into the cave. As the boy shined the light against the walls of the cave, he saw all of the gold that was stuck in the walls.

"Eureka!" exclaimed the boy. "We have found the mother lode."

The boy's father and mother came rushing into the cave and saw all of the gold. "Bonanza!" they all yelled at the top of their lungs. The boy and his family were very happy. Opie was also very happy for the boy and his family. He joined in the celebration by cheering and yelling "Bonanza" at the top of his lungs and dancing around.

The boy and his family, with the help of Opie, mined the cave until all of the gold was found. They had fun mining the cave for gold and passed the time by singing folk songs. Once all of the gold was mined, the boy and his family decided that it was time to head back to their home in Virginia. They had been gone for a real long time and were homesick for their friends and family. They packed up all of their supplies and loaded the gold into their wagon. After several months of traveling, the boy, his family, and Opie returned home. They were warmly greeted by everyone in the town. They boy and his family told everyone

of their adventure, showing them some of the gold that they had discovered. The boy and his family had more gold than they needed, so they shared their good fortune with their friends. There was even enough gold left over for Opie. This made Opie very happy.

It was getting late and the sun was starting to set over the horizon. Opie had been away from his forest for a very long time, and he really missed his home. "I think it is time for me to head back home," said Opie. Before he began his journey home, Opie crawled up the boy's back porch. He wanted to make sure that the boy and his family were safely back inside their home. He looked through the door and softly said, "Goodbye." He thought about all of the fun he had had with the boy and about how much he had discovered about America. Opie put his gold in a little brown sack and carried it on his back so he could share it with all of his woodland friends. And with that, Opie turned and walked back into the woods signing "Oh My Darlin' Clementine," thinking about the new adventure he would have the next time he returned to the boy's home.

THE END

A POSSUM'S GOLD RUSH LESSON

The gold rush in California was called the "California Dream." This dream eventually spread across America and became part of what is known as the "American Dream." Thirty-thousand people journeyed to California in search of gold and a new life. This was one of the largest voluntary migrations in the history of the United States. The California Gold Rush lasted roughly ten years. Approximately four hundred sixty-five million dollars in gold was unearthed during this time period.

Even though lots of gold was discovered, it only led to great wealth for a very few people. Many people returned to their homes with nothing more than what they started out with. With the migration to California, San Francisco and other towns grew from tiny little settlements into boomtowns. The finding of gold by the pioneers, also known as the "forty-niners" since they mined for gold in 1849, helped California to become a state in 1850. The gold rush also helped America to grow and expand as a country. New agriculture flourished in California, and new forms of transportation were built to connect all of America. These new types of transportation included railroads and steamships. They were used to transport people and supplies from coast to coast and "sea to shining sea."

However, the California Gold Rush was not all positive for the United States. Due to the greed of some Americans, the Native Americans were attacked and were forced off of their promised land. The peace agreement between the Native Americans and the people of America was broken and has never been fully mended. Finally, the continued mining and excavation of gold and other natural resources over the last hundred years has caused severe environmental damage to the earth. If this continues, it could have the potential to cause serious harm to the earth that cannot be corrected or undone.

listen|imagine|view|experience

AUDIO BOOK DOWNLOAD INCLUDED WITH THIS BOOK!

In your hands you hold a complete digital entertainment package. Besides purchasing the paper version of this book, this book includes a free download of the audio version of this book. Simply use the code listed below when visiting our website. Once downloaded to your computer, you can listen to the book through your computer's speakers, burn it to an audio CD or save the file to your portable music device (such as Apple's popular iPod) and listen on the go!

How to get your free audio book digital download:

1. Visit www.tatepublishing.com and click on the e|LIVE logo on the home page.
2. Enter the following coupon code:
   158e-4e83-16cd-30d4-660c-b14e-558c-630d
3. Download the audio book from your e|LIVE digital locker and begin enjoying your new digital entertainment package today!